The heroic deeds of

BEOWULF

retold by Gladys Schmitt

ILLUSTRATED BY WALTER FERRO

RANDOM HOUSE · NEW YORK

LEGACY

BOOKS

To my godson,
DAVID STRAUSS

OF THE BUILDING OF HEOROT AND THE COMING OF THE MONSTER GRENDEL

In those days it was no small thing to build a house. There was plenty of timber in the ancient forests of pine and beeches. But there were no saws, only iron axes for hacking the hard trunks. Whatever had to be taken from one place to another could only be rolled or dragged by men.

So when Hrothgar, king of the Danes, said he would build a splendid house, larger than any that men had ever seen, there was much labor and sweat for his servants and companions. The snowy forests rang long with the sounds of axes and the crash of mighty trees. And by night the anvils sang and the fires of the smithies reddened the northern skies. For King Hrothgar commanded these smiths to make iron bands to bind the hall without and within, so that no outburst of quarreling inside or storm or assault outside could pull the royal building down.

King Hrothgar built his hall in a time of peace to celebrate his many victories. He was in the flower of his age, blond and straight and comely. And even his fair wife Wealhtheow could not find a single strand of gray in his yellow beard and hair.

"We will build the hall," he said to his thanes who had helped him fight his battles, "on a hill close to the town, a little away from the unhealthy mists of the fens and marshes, and not too far from the sea. There every evening, while peace and my riches last, we will all feast and drink mead together. The minstrels will sing, and I will give rich gifts to those of you who do great deeds and are kind and brave."

So the hall was built, and speedily, too, because the warrior-thanes loved their king and had nothing against feasting and drinking every night. It was indeed the finest and largest hall that Danish eyes had ever looked upon, big enough to hold warriors by the hundred. There were two great entrances, one at each end. And the doors were bound with strips of wrought iron and set on enormous hinges and fastened with iron locks and clasps. The roof was high and gabled, and outside, on the front gable, King Hrothgar had them fasten the antlers of a deer that he himself had

4

caught. He called his hall "The Deer," which, in their ancient language, was "Heorot."

The great hall Heorot was divided by pillars into three aisles, and the three aisles were furnished with three big tables and six long benches, so that all the warriors who followed King Hrothgar could sit down at one time. The King's bench was in the middle, and the floor there was raised. And there was a high throne at one end of that middle bench for King Hrothgar and Queen Wealhtheow. The Queen and her ladies had woven beautiful tapestries to cover the raw timber of the walls, tapestries embroidered in scarlet and blue and gold with scenes of the King's victories.

Torches were lighted when the sun went down, and firelight flickered on the tapestries and on the ring-mail corselets of the warrior-guests and on their metal drinking cups. The minstrels sang about old battles, and Hrothgar and Wealhtheow left their high seat and walked among their guests, giving gifts and praise. Never had there been a better, happier time in the land of the Danes.

But all could not go well forever, even in so fine a place as Heorot. Those who came there to drink mead and feast never came by way of the unwholesome fens and marshes. There was an evil smell over that way, and a sound of troubled waters, and a mist that never cleared even at high noon. And now and again a farmer who had lost a sheep would follow it to the edge of the fen and come home very pale.

"You know," the farmer would say to his goodwife, "over by the fen I saw a dreadful thing. A monster, a giant, a tremendous thing, neither man nor bear—I cannot say what it was—came splashing and hulking toward me out of the evil waters."

And the goodwife, half scornful and half believing, would ask her husband, "And where is our sheep?"

And the husband would answer, shaking, "In the gullet of that monster, I suppose. All I could find on the muddy bank was a little heap of bones picked clean and a dribble of blood."

It became known in that neighborhood that there were *two* who lived under the troubled water, this same monster and his mother, a giantess with fangs and claws and wild, wet hair. Sometimes they would be seen stalking around the fen land or walking through the thick, dark, misty forest together. Then men would call home their flocks, and women would sleep with their arms around their children, fearful of the monster Grendel and his mother, whom they called "Grendel's Dame."

Now, until the time we tell of, Grendel had never feasted on men or women or children. All

he had dared to drag down into the marsh were horses or sheep. But in his cold, dank home at the bottom of the fen water, night after night he heard the joyful sounds at King Hrothgar's hall. They floated down to him, the laughing and the jesting and the songs of the minstrel. And his blood boiled with anger at the noise of men's pleasure, for he had a dark and furious heart in his hairy chest.

"I will give them reason to howl," he thought in his rage and his loneliness. "I will put a stop to their laughter and their singing!"

Then, one black winter's night, the awful thing came about. The monster Grendel swam up from his home at the bottom of the fen and splashed through the marshes and came to Heorot.

With a mere tug of his claws he broke open the door, wrenching the hinges, snapping the iron bolts. The warriors slept on fine cushions near their feasting places on the benches. Their helmets and ring-mail corselets lay on their seats above them. Their swords and round shields stood against the wall. But their weapons did them no good. The warriors were heavy with mead and meat and did not waken. While they slept, the monster Grendel snatched up and carried off thirty noble thanes. And nothing more was ever heard of them, except that those who went to the fen to look for them saw a terrible change in the troubled waters. The lake was purple-red instead of brown. The uneasy waves were colored with human blood.

There were some then who would not sleep at Heorot. And two nights after the slaughter the monster came again. This time he took even more from among those who had been brave enough to lie down there to rest. After that, no man, not even the good King Hrothgar, dared to make merry in the mead hall. It stood empty and hollow, silent, without laughter or music. The iron bands rusted, and cobwebs gathered on the ceiling and spiders spun webs on the walls.

Nor was the giant Grendel satisfied, for now he was always thirsty for human blood. He stalked through farm and village, snatching up one man here and another there. The whole land was afraid. As for the fine mead hall Heorot, it was a cause for shame to King Hrothgar and his thanes. No man dared to defend it against Grendel. Every warrior accused himself of cowardice. And the good king grew old with sorrow. Queen Wealhtheow, no matter how hard she looked, could not find one gold thread left in his silver beard and hair.

9

Of THE COURAGE OF
THE YOUNG PAGE BEOWULF

Whatever is too much for the old to look after should be taken over by the young. Many a boy in the Daneland grew to manhood while King Hrothgar grieved, but none was brave enough to face Grendel in the hall. The shameful story was carried over the frozen water to the neighboring land of the Geats. There was a young king there named Hygelac. But when he heard he only sighed and shook his head. Hygelac had a fair new bride called Hygd whom he did not wish to leave. Besides, he had to defend his own land against enemy warriors and fierce sea serpents that came inland out of the deep.

So Hygelac said no more than this: "It is a great pity. Perhaps some day one of my pages—young Breca, here, or Beowulf—will grow up and take a foamy-necked ship across the water. Perhaps Breca—or even Beowulf—will be the one to avenge Hrothgar and cleanse his hall."

Now, of the two lads named by Hygelac, king of the Geats, Beowulf was the stronger and the more comely. He was broad of shoulder and narrow of waist and thigh. His muscles were as hard as iron in his sunburned arms. His grip was like steel. His eyes were clear gray and his hair was reddish gold. But King Hygelac thought less of him than of his fellow page, the black-haired Breca. And here is the reason that it was always Breca, never Beowulf, who rode with King Hygelac and carried the jeweled mead cup for the fair young Queen Hygd:

Beowulf and Breca were the best of swimmers, and no man could tell which was the better of the two. So once in winter, when the ice floats were crowding the gray-green waters, they took it into their heads to test their skills. It was a friendly match, for the lads were good companions. The water was filled with whales and sea serpents, so they plunged in armed in their ring-mesh coats of mail, each of the lads with his sword in his hand. Fearful of the sea beasts and fond of each other, they swam close together, side by side, for five nights in the icy sea. Then the sea tide parted them, the seething billows came between them. Darkest night came down, and Beowulf was alone.

11

The sea creatures sensed that there was human flesh in the water. The scent of the swimmer stirred them up and they came after him, nipped at him, thrust at him with their tusks, tried to coil around him. But his chain mail saved him, and he kept them off with his sword.

Then one great spotty monster snatched at him and dragged him down and down to the floor of the ocean. Others of the same kind came to help, hoping to have a taste of human flesh. But Beowulf, weary as he was, thrust right and left with his keen blade and fought free of them all, and came up, just as morning broke, to the top of the waves. Nine sea serpents he killed. He counted their bodies floating upside down on the dark water. These nine would never creep to shore to threaten men again, or come snorting at ships and crack them to bits.

Beowulf had done well ridding the world of these hateful pests, but Breca had won the swimming match. Long before Beowulf struggled onto the windy cliffs which they had left together, Breca had reached the goal on the opposite shore.

So Hygelac, king of the Geats, and his young Queen Hygd praised Breca much and put Beowulf always in second place. And Beowulf bore it well, saying nothing. But sometimes it stuck him like a

thorn in his chest, especially since he loved Hygelac like a father. His own brave father was dead.

Now, one night in early spring, when Hygelac's
thanes, young and old, sat late by the fire talking
of Hrothgar's woes, a great thought came like a
flash of summer lightning into the mind of young
Beowulf. "I am strong, and I have a braver spirit
than they know here in Geatland," he thought. "I
will go and help Hrothgar and give him back his
great hall Heorot. For honor and for pity I will
do it, and ask for no reward except a kind word
from my own king and queen." And at once,
while his heart and hopes were high, he went
around Hygelac's hall and asked his young companions to come with him. Nor did those friends
fail him. Fourteen promised to sail in a carved
boat across the sea and to fight Grendel at Beowulf's side, even to the death.

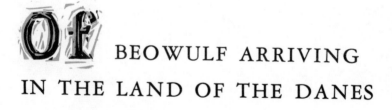 BEOWULF ARRIVING
IN THE LAND OF THE DANES

The light wind drove them over the springtime
water. The ship met no misfortune. She flew to

13

Daneland like a bird. There on the coast of Hrothgar's kingdom, on the beach under the gray cliffs, they took their weapons out of the vessel and gave thanks to God who had brought them there so luckily and so soon.

But they had scarcely unloaded when King

Hrothgar's coast warden rode down to them. He had seen their shields and mail coats gleaming from his post on the cliffs above them, and feared they were enemies. His lean face was grim between his brown beard and his bright helmet. "For a long time I have stood guard on these cliffs," he said, "and no band of armed men has dared to land as openly as you. It will be best for you to tell me quickly what your business is in the land of my king."

Then Beowulf spoke like a determined captain, young though he was. "We come as friends from the land of the Geats," he said. "I am Beowulf, and my father was the famed warrior Ecgtheow. He did high deeds before death called him out of our house. His name is known throughout the world. Our errand is a blameless one. We are here to save King Hrothgar from shame, to cleanse his mead hall and ease his woes. Do not hold us

here or turn us back. We bring with us better days for the warrior-Danes."

Then the grim warden smiled, for the young warrior was frank and fine to look upon. Courteously he rode before the strangers to show them the way to Hrothgar's hall. When they caught sight of its gleaming roof from the cliffs, he told them to march on without him. He did not dare to leave his post. His eyes were keen for enemies. And they went, fifteen good Geatish warriors in marching order, their soles ringing on the stones of the path, their swords and shields gleaming, their mail coats jingling, until they came to the broad terrace around the splendid hall.

There they were questioned by Hrothgar's herald and told to wait. And Beowulf could scarcely bear the waiting—there was such a longing in him to see the King. Because a stranger had come to him from a far land, Hrothgar decided to meet him in a stately fashion in the great hall, even though it had long stood neglected and unused. The King sat now with a few of his faithful Danes around him. And, when he had taken his place on his high seat, the herald came out and invited the stranger to follow him in.

Shadowy it was, and sorrowful, too, in that mead chamber. There was a smell of dampness there, and slants of sunshine showed the ruin—the cobwebs, the dusty benches, the wrenched locks and hinges, the great iron bands reddened here and there by rust. Alone on his high seat, with his warriors at his feet, sat the good King Hrothgar. His beard and hair were fine and silvery like the webs spun by spiders. His face was netted over with countless wrinkles. His eyes, blue and faded, looked at the lad who had come so far across the sea.

He asked in a gentle voice who Beowulf was. He said, after he was told, that he had known the lad's father and mother. "And what do you mean to do for me?" he asked. "Surely you are not so reckless that you and your little band will sleep under this accursed roof and meet the monster Grendel here by night?"

Then Beowulf told him that he meant to do exactly that. And the lad looked so strong and tall, and his voice sounded with so brave a note that the tired king began to take heart. "Heaven bless you for your courage and your kindness," he said, and embraced the stranger as though he were a son. "You see how it is with me. My warrior band is ruined by Grendel. He has carried off many to their deaths and has frozen the hearts of the rest with fear. We can do nothing against

17

him. Only God can deliver us, and it may be that you are sent by God."

At this all the Danish warriors nodded—all except one. That one, whose face was dark and sour, frowned at the young man. He was Hrothgar's favorite, and his name was Unferth. He sat closest to the high seat with his head near the King's knee. Black jealousy rose in him when he saw another man ready to do what he would not do himself.

King Hrothgar said, "The brave guests are weary and hungry. Clear a bench and bring them mead and meat. Call in a minstrel to sing of old, brave deeds. Such songs will give them courage and faith in themselves."

So a bench was cleared and a minstrel was summoned, and the kind Queen Wealhtheow came from her bower to honor the feast. For the first time in many years, merry noises sounded in Heorot. The meat was tasty and crisp, and the mead was pure nectar poured from a great jeweled cup. And the sight of the old king's happiness was so dear to Beowulf that he felt no fear, felt only a strong need to make his host happier still.

Then the sour-faced Unferth raised his voice and called from his seat of honor to Beowulf. "Are you not that Beowulf who had a reckless swimming match with Breca?" he asked. "I have heard that you two risked your lives like fools in the winter waters. I have heard also that Breca beat you at it roundly. *He* reached the goal, but *you* came back to shore a sorry sight."

Beowulf's throat tightened at that taunt. He longed to hurl his beaker at Unferth. But he mastered himself and said with dignity: "It is true that we were reckless, but we were only young pages then. It is also true that he reached the goal and I did not, though no man in Geatland would mock me for that. They know the truth. Ask, and they will tell you I slew nine sea monsters under the icy water. Ask, and they will tell you they are grateful to me, glad that these beasts I killed will never creep onto the shore or fall upon their boats and drag the mariners down to be eaten under the sea. Also, let me tell you this: If *you* were a man of courage, your king would not have grown old with grieving. *You* would have killed Grendel and cleansed his hall."

Once he had said it, he feared he had displeased the good Hrothgar. But the King only smiled, and Unferth blushed and held his tongue.

Then the minstrel struck up another song, and the merry noises rose again—the sound of the harp, the talk, and the laughter. The kind Queen

19

Wealhtheow, faded by trouble but still beautiful in her embroidered robes and golden diadem, came down from the high seat. It was her custom to offer the jeweled cup of mead first to the King and then to his guests. When she brought the cup to Beowulf, she spoke to him in a clear voice. "I thank God that what I have hoped for is about to come to pass. I believe that you, dear stranger, will deliver us from our woes," she said.

And before he took the cup from her, Beowulf answered her with these words: "Lady, before I stepped from the shore of Geatland I had promised myself that one of two things would become of me. Either I would slay the monster or meet my death at grips with him in your husband's hall."

Then the noise of the feast slowly lessened, though it was still loud enough to reach the ears of Grendel under the loathsome fen water. The Queen went away to her bower, and the King followed her, and all the Danish warriors bade the strangers good night and went to sleep in some safer place.

With the others gone, the band of Geatish warriors seemed small. The light of day was quenched, and the torches died out. Beowulf's companions slept on cushions. They set their helmets on the benches above them, but wore their coats of mail and kept their swords under their hands. Beowulf did otherwise. He gave his mail and helmet, his sword and spear to a companion. "I will not make a shameful thing of the high arts of battle by using them against such a foul creature," he said. "Grendel uses no weapons, and neither will I. I will overcome him as he will strive to overcome me, with nothing but the might of my body and the grip of my naked hands."

It was no easy thing to fall asleep in the echoing blackness. Not one of them hoped to see again his people at home, his castle where he had been brought up, or the dear coast of his native land.

Of BEOWULF GRAPPLING WITH THE MONSTER, AND THE REJOICING AT HEOROT

Then came Grendel in the dim night, splashing through the fen waters, tearing like a high wind through the black forests. He was headed for Heorot, and all there had fallen asleep—all but one!

Beowulf, wide-eyed on his pillow, heard the thudding feet, saw the big door fly open. The tremendous and horrible shape, the hairy creature, half man, half beast, showed in the doorway in the light of the misted moon. His eyes shone red, like murky fire. He laughed aloud to see such a fine feast, and the laugh was so dreadful that it froze even the hero's heart.

Before Beowulf could recover his courage, the monstrous paw of the man-beast snatched up the closest warrior, clawed him, tore him, flung him back onto the floor, his life's blood drained away. Then it reached again for the next of the good companions, but by this time Beowulf had himself in hand. He sprang up and gripped the devilish creature's paw. For the first time, Grendel felt terror. Never in his evil life had he felt such a grip. There was no courage in him when he was brought to the test. At once he tried to get away, but no matter how hard he shook and dragged he could not pull loose from the iron-strong hand.

Then the young hero did not fear the foul breath and the fiery eyes. He did not seek to keep himself from the hairy beast. He grappled with

the creature brow to brow and knee to knee. And their grappling was so fierce that they turned over benches and cracked wall timbers and pillars.

By this time the others were awake. Armed, they came to their chieftain's help, laying about them in the blackness with swords. But swords could do nothing against the monster. Only the grip of Beowulf, still holding him fast, could bring him harm.

In that grip Grendel threw himself about so wildly that it was a wonder he did not bring Heorot down. Surely the hall would have been shattered if it had not been held by the iron bands. And, just as Beowulf began to feel mortal weariness, just as the flesh began to split at his knuckles from the hardness of his grip, the monster uttered a blood-freezing yell. A crack had opened in Grendel's shoulder. The sinews there sprang wide. The covering of his bones spread apart. Shrieking, he pulled himself free and fled into the night. But he left something behind him. His hairy paw, his forearm, his upper arm as high as the shoulder remained at Heorot, held fast in Beowulf's gripping hand.

That gruesome trophy made Beowulf rejoice. With such a wound in his shoulder, it was plain that Grendel could not live to bring sorrow to the

Danes. The young hero hung the arm of the monster beneath the antlers under the gable. Then he and his comrades lay down among the broken benches and shattered tables and slept.

That was a happy morning for the Danes. They rode out to follow the track of Grendel to the fens. They saw the lake blood-tinged again, but this time there was no weeping at the sight. Farmers and townsmen and warriors need no longer fear that their kinsmen's blood would stain the muddy waters. Women and children could stay out of doors in the evening and sleep fearlessly through the night.

The Danish warriors rode back to Heorot, praising Beowulf all the way. They said that he was like the greatest of their ancient heroes, the dragon-slaying Siegmund. In the pale light of the spring dawning they spurred their horses for pure joy and raced each other on the new green turf. Truly, the stranger from afar had brought better days for the Danes!

None cared to remember then that *two* had lived under the brown waters. Their minds were set on merrier matters—feasting and gift-giving to celebrate the victory. By midafternoon, Queen Wealhtheow and her ladies had hung the splendid tapestries

25

and set three tables that creaked under their loads of burnished plates and jeweled cups. By dusk all the warriors, Danes and Geats, had assembled at Heorot to share in the rejoicing. Beowulf was summoned to sit with King Hrothgar in a place as honorable as Unferth's. Never did a gladder king more richly entertain a more welcome and beloved guest.

These are the gifts that the generous King Hrothgar gave to Beowulf the Geat while they sat at meat and mead, while the minstrel sang and all the warriors were glad in their hearts that Grendel could no longer hear:

A golden banner on a great staff of ash wood
A helmet with a charging golden boar on its crest

- A great sword, very ancient, with a beautifully carved hilt
- Eight horses, all with braided golden reins
- A saddle of silver on which Hrothgar had himself ridden to battle
- A coat of mail made all of silver rings

All these he gave to Beowulf, and with them much gold to be carried back to the kinsfolk of the good warrior whom Grendel had slain. The eight horses were brought by squires straight into the hall, where they snorted and pawed the paved floor. To each of the thirteen remaining companions, the King also gave a gift, such a precious one as to make a man proud for all of his days.

Beowulf valued his gifts, but he valued them less than the King's hand on his shoulder, the King's kind eyes on his face. Dear to him too, and dearer than any gift, were Hrothgar's wise words:

"Be as a son to me now, dear Beowulf. Let my children be your brothers and my wife be your mother. Let peace last forever and good will never cease between the Kingdom of the Geats and the Kingdom of the Danes."

As for Unferth, his taunting tongue was silent. He boasted no more, though there was as yet no love for Beowulf in his heart.

Then came Queen Wealhtheow again from the high seat to offer the guests her hospitable cup. Having first served her lord and told him to rejoice in his good fortune, she went next to Beowulf. To him she, too, gave priceless presents: two bracelets of twisted gold, a mantle woven by her own hand, many broad gold rings, and a necklace finer than any on earth, all of hammered gold set with gleaming and costly stones.

After that, the minstrel sang again until the Geats, still worn from the night's battle, began to show a yearning for sleep. Then the King invited them to lie down on soft pillows in another place, and the Danish thanes prepared themselves to sleep in the mead hall Heorot and to guard it as they had not dared to guard it these many years.

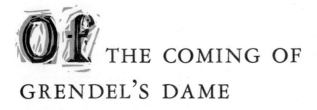 THE COMING OF GRENDEL'S DAME

That blessed sleep was brief for Beowulf. He was wakened at dawning by the sound of wild wailing and brought at once to the King, where he sat in

Queen Wealhtheow's bower. He knew in an instant by Hrothgar's wet eyes and bowed shoulders that Heorot was not cleansed, that the evil days for the Danes could not yet be counted in the past. Hrothgar, weeping, told him the whole unhappy tale:

The water hag, the second of those who lived under the lake in the fenland, had come to take vengeance for the slaying of her son Grendel. While the Danish warriors had slept she had come stealthily into the mead hall and had snatched up and carried away the King's dear counselor, whom no man could hope to look upon again on earth. It was as it had been before Beowulf came to Daneland. The path from Heorot to the fen was dribbled with human blood.

Others came, too, to the Queen's bower. Among them was Unferth, jealous no more. He had wakened too late to save the noble victim, but early enough to see the fiery eyes and yellow fangs of Grendel's mother gleaming in the dark. He knew now what Beowulf had borne and was still to bear.

For the young hero said to Hrothgar, "Do not mourn, beloved King. It is better to avenge the death of a friend than to weep for him. Only show me the way to the fen where the water hag dwells, and I will make an end of her there or come to a brave end myself."

As he spoke, it was hard for him not to weep. For his mind flew to his own land, to King Hygelac and the fair Queen Hygd, who as yet knew nothing of what he had brought about in the land of the Danes. He yearned to have them know how he had earned the right to their respect by wrestling with Grendel. He wished to show them the gifts that King Hrothgar and Queen Wealhtheow had given to him at the feasting, to let them see that he was not given a second place in the country of the Danes.

"But before I go," he said to King Hrothgar, "promise me that you will send the matchless gifts that you gave me to the King and the Queen of the Geats if I do not come back out of the fen. Then, even if I am dead, they will know that I did brave deeds in another country, and found there a loving and generous lord and a gracious lady, and had reason to be happy in the short while I lived."

The King freely promised. Unferth, ashamed of his hatefulness, unbuckled from his side his own sword, a priceless and ancient one, and gave it to Beowulf to use against Grendel's Dame. All thirteen of the Geats and a great company of the

Danes offered to ride with the young hero to the edge of the lake. So they set out, grim and silent, and followed the bloody path past the town and into the wilderness. And the land they traveled was a misty and eerie land.

It was a country seldom visited by human kind. There were crags where the wolf walked, and windy cliffs, and great steaming waterfalls. On the other side of these there was a forest, still wintry though the rest of the country was green with spring. Twisted trees joined ash-gray limbs with one another, and the dried leaves rattled and were whitened by everlasting frost. This forest grew to the very edge of the evil lake—its roots showed interlocked under the muddy, blood-stained waves. It was told by the Danes how a deer, if a hunter pursued it to this lake, would stand and die on the edge of it rather than wade in. On the yellow bank were the strange, misshapen footprints of Grendel's Dame, and here the heartsick warriors sat down to wait.

"Stay by me here, for I may yet return," said Beowulf. "I and I alone will go down into the water, to meet and struggle with her as I struggled with the sea serpents in my match with Breca long ago. If the water hag has the better of me, no man will see me again, and the good

32

King Hrothgar will not have the trouble of giving
me a funeral or building me a burial mound.
And I will know as I am dying that the King
of the Danes will keep his faith with me. Those
who came here with me he will send back safely

to their homes. And the gifts that I received from him and Wealhtheow he will send to King Hygelac and Queen Hygd."

Then he put on his coat of mail and took Unferth's sword in his hand and leaped into the loathsome lake. Those who had ridden there with him, Danes and Geats alike, sat grimly on the black rocks, biting their lips to keep from weeping. For they had come to love him well for his courage and his frank ways and his comely body and his kindliness, and there was not one in all the company who hoped to set eyes on him again.

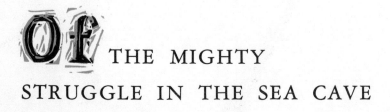 THE MIGHTY
STRUGGLE IN THE SEA CAVE

The foul lake seemed bottomless. It was close to noon before Beowulf came close to the last level of it. Sea creatures stopped him on the way, but he did not fear them. After the swimming match with Breca, he knew they had no power against his coat of mail. Down near the sandy floor the water was clearer, and he could see strange polished stones and shimmering lights and gray shadows. He caught sight of her then—the water hag, Grendel's mother. She came swimming toward him through the weird light, her eyes and fangs gleaming, her hair spread wild and dark on the tide.

She grabbed for him, caught him at once, held him between her clawed hands. She squeezed him so hard he feared she would press the life out of his chest. But his skin at least was safe. She could not pierce the mail coat even with her sharp claws. Her strength was less than Grendel's, and Beowulf might even have broken her grasp and drawn Unferth's sword against her if he had not been so harried by the serpents that swam to her help, coiling and flapping against him and nipping at his face.

He knew then that she was carrying him off over the sanded bottom of the lake. She bore him through dark and narrow passages between high cliffs of gray stone. Still holding him, she knocked a great, slimy door open with her shoulders. Into her mansion under the fen water she dragged him, and there he breathed again, for there was no water in the place. The whole weight of the lake was held off by the stone roof and walls. The door banged shut after them, and there was

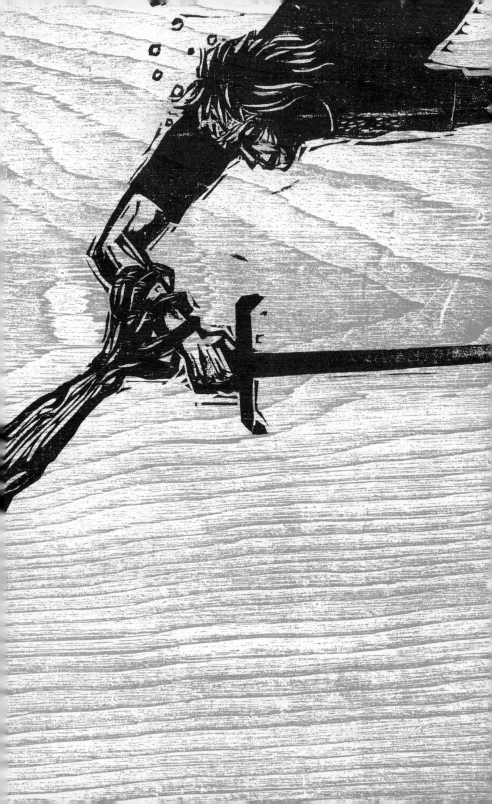

darkness all around, broken only by the yellow gleam of an eerie fire.

Now that his feet were solid on the paved floor of her mansion, Beowulf heaved hard and broke her grasp. Quickly he went at her evil head with Unferth's sword. But that ancient blade, trusty as it had proved itself in the world of men, was useless here. It rang again and again on her head but made no cut, and at last he threw it aside. Once again, he knew, he must trust to his own strength. He grappled with the mother as he had grappled with the son, brow to brow and knee to knee. She was weaker than he had expected—the force in her was less than half the force of Grendel. And after a short struggle, he toppled her backward onto the floor.

But then he was seized by mortal weariness from wrestling and long swimming and the weight of the water that had pressed for hours upon him. He grew dizzy and passed his hand over his eyes, and when he took it away he saw that she was up again and coming at him with a flashing blade. Easily she flung him backward and sat on his legs, thrusting at him again and again with her short evil knife. He had reason to be thankful then for his ringed mail coat. Without that good armor, he would surely have been stabbed to death.

Suddenly, while she thrust at him and he gasped for breath, the eerie yellow fire flared up and he saw, hanging on the wall of that vast room, a tremendous sword with a bright blade and a golden hilt. Hope strengthened him then. He heaved her up, struggled from under her, pushed

her aside. He darted past her and grasped the giant's weapon by its precious hilt.

She cringed, and he struck her with fury full on the neck. Her black blood spurted out—*this* sword had power to pierce her hide. She fell at once and died without a sound. "So," he said to himself, "even if it should not be granted to me to rise from this lake and see the sky again, both of the evil ones are taken from the earth, and I will be remembered in the songs of the Danes."

He wandered about in her dark and secret mansion, with Unferth's sword in his left hand and the giant blade in his right. The firelight grew still brighter. He could make out treasure heaps and many ancient weapons and grisly piles of the bones of beasts and men. In his wanderings he came upon a bed, and on that bed was the body of the dead Grendel. With the tremendous sword he smote off the monster's head, and the blood gushed out and ran over the floor and between the door and the doorsill, so that the water beyond the door was stained purplish red.

Then the strangest event in all that strange adventure came about: So poisonous was the gore of Grendel that the giant blade began to melt away under the red stain. As ice melts under the spring wind, as frost melts in the sun, so the steel melted. It dripped away until only the hilt was left, precious and weighty, encrusted with rare jewels and plated in polished gold. Though there were many rare weapons and much ancient jewelry in that mansion under the evil lake, this only did Beowulf bear away with him to the world of men —the hilt of the sword with which he had avenged King Hrothgar's sorrows and washed out the shame of the Danes.

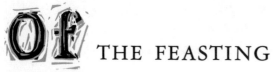 THE FEASTING AT HEOROT

Now it was late in the afternoon, and those who sat waiting by the lake under the wintry trees felt their hopes draining away. Fear had come upon them when they saw the water churned up by the struggle between Grendel's Dame and the Geatish hero. Despair possessed them utterly when they saw the muddy water purpled again with blood. There not one among them who hoped to see the dear deliverer swim out of those evil waves. They saw no cause to wait. They thought it would be best to comfort themselves before the fires of their homes, for there was still a touch of chill in the spring air.

First the Danish thanes departed, getting wearily onto their horses and riding away with bent necks. Then, after long waiting alone, Beowulf's own good companions also heaved themselves up from the dreary bank with sighs. The last and most faithful of these was departing when he heard a splash in the fen and looked over his shoulder. Then he saw—and his heart leaped up at the sight—his brave lord Beowulf wading toward the shore. Sturdy and unharmed the hero had come up out of the dreadful depths, with Unferth's sword and the golden hilt of the great one he had found in the mansion below.

And now that he was restored to his comrades, the wintry woodland echoed with merry shouts, with the blowing of horns, with the thud of feet as men came running to tell the Danes and King Hrothgar that what they had feared had not come about. There was a great bustle in Heorot at the good tidings. Queen Wealhtheow and her ladies laid out fresh garments for Beowulf, a tunic of the finest linen and an embroidered scarlet cloak. The table was set for the most splendid of all the feasts. Bread baked in the ovens, and meat sizzled

42

over the fire, and the best mead was brought, and the jeweled beakers were filled to the brim with the honey-sweet drink. Every minstrel within call was summoned to come at once with his harp. The most fearful of all the warriors who gathered there knew now that he had nothing to fear. The good days had truly come at last for King Hrothgar and his Danes.

At that feast, Beowulf was the gift-giver. To the old king he gave the hilt of the giant's sword, encrusted with enough precious metal to ransom ten kings. He would not take it home with him to Geatland, though it would have made a great name for him among his fellow warriors there. It seemed better to him that it should remain as a trophy in Heorot, to make King Hrothgar think kindly of him when he was gone.

To Unferth he returned the other blade, thanking him courteously and saying nothing against it. Though it had failed him in the dreadful time when the sea hag had pressed him hard, still it had been offered to him in good faith and with good intent. For that reason he called it a noble blade before the Danes and the Geats and said that its equal would be hard to find. Nor could Unferth think otherwise than well of a man who

43

had treated him so courteously and done two such deeds for his king and his native land.

Beowulf felt then such happiness as he had never known, sitting on the raised floor near the King's high seat with his head close to Hrothgar's knee. A blessed sleepiness numbed him. The warmth of the mead moved through his blood. He was weary with the weight of the fen water and the long battle with Grendel's Dame. Then, too, his body was light and comfortable with satisfaction. He had undertaken a great labor and finished it in glory. When a man knows that he has done well, heaven gives him the sweetest and soundest rest.

For a long time that night he sat listening to the minstrels and talking with the King and feeling Hrothgar's hand fall in gratefulness and blessing on his head. Then, in his sleepiness, visions began to form between him and the torches and the bright coats of mail before him. He saw his own castle, where he had been raised. He saw the beautiful mead hall of the King of the Geats, not so large as Heorot, but broad enough and crowded with faces that he knew and loved. He saw, too, visions of the handsome young King Hygelac and the golden-haired Queen Hygd. "We must not feast with you too late tonight," he said to Hrothgar. "Early tomorrow we must leave our beds and load our boat and start for home."

Then King Hrothgar, sad to part with so dear a deliverer, gave him what is more to be valued than arms and jewels and horses. A king's advice he gave him, speaking out of the wisdom of his age. These precepts he gave to Beowulf, to guide him through the rest of his days. And there was not one of them that the young hero forgot.

"In the years of your greatness—for you will be great—do not be puffed up and proud," said King Hrothgar. "Do not be grasping or over-bearing with your thanes. Whatever they help you to win in war, divide freely and graciously with them. Make many fine feasts in your own castle in Geatland, and pass out all good things without stinting to your guests—armor and chargers and precious rings. If you live in this manner, when sorrow comes upon you, you will have a companion to share it. And when you no longer walk on the earth, you will be praised by minstrels and remembered for a thousand years."

After that, King Hrothgar embraced and kissed Beowulf and called him his own dear son. The King and Unferth and Queen Wealhtheow and all the others who had come to love the stranger

45

clasped hands with him and wept that he should depart so soon, and wished him well. Then the Geats went to the embroidered pillows and coverlets that had been prepared for them by the Queen and her ladies, and the Danes lay down in Heorot. Nor was there anything left under the star-studded heavens to trouble their sweet sleep.

OF THE RETURN TO GEATLAND

That was a happy journey. The boat was twice as heavy as it had been when they had come to Daneland. The eight noble horses stamped in it, and prow and stern were crowded with Hrothgar's gifts of arms and gold. But the spring winds drove it lightly over the foamy sea. The warriors sang as they dipped their oars in the spring-blue water. They made new songs about Beowulf and Grendel and Beowulf and Grendel's Dame. And they sang loudest when they saw the gray cliffs of their native land rising above the waves.

Hygelac, King of the Geats, was in his mead

hall distributing rings. He saw from his window the fire lighted by his coast warden—the fire that told him the wanderers had come back home. At once he summoned his fair young queen and told her to deck the hall so that Beowulf and his thanes might be given a proper welcome. Here, too, mead and meat were set out by the white hands of ladies, and minstrels were called in to hear with their own ears the great deeds that they would later turn into songs.

It took the heroes a long time to come up from the coast. Though the way was short, they had much to carry. Weighted down with gifts they entered the mead hall of King Hygelac. They led in the eight splendid horses with their reins of braided gold. They carried the golden banner before them. They made a great heap of rich things—mail coats and helmets, bracelets and rings—in a corner on the floor. King Hygelac looked on with wonder. Breca also was among those who had come to the welcoming, and he embraced and praised the famed warrior who had once been his fellow page.

Beowulf mounted to the raised place where King Hygelac sat, and waited for his lord to ask him to tell his story. Then he spoke as the good King Hrothgar would have had him speak, simply and with modesty. He was not proud or puffed up. He had no need to boast. The truth was great enough. He was grateful to God, also, that he had lived to tell this tale in the mead hall of the Geats. All that he had dreamed of in Daneland was here before him now for his eyes to see and his hands to touch. And he thought that, of all the lands in the world, the homeland is always the best.

While Beowulf spoke of Grendel and Grendel's Dame, King Hygelac's blue eyes shone upon him, as the eyes of a proud father might shine. Queen Hygd, even more lovely than he had remembered her, smiled at him and took his hand in her fair hand. "Beowulf," she said when he was finished, "you have done enough in Daneland to keep our minstrels singing for a hundred years."

Nor did he forget King Hrothgar's advice that the warrior should be generous. The best of his rewards he gave to those that he most loved. To King Hygelac he gave four of the beautiful horses and the silver coat of mail and the fine gold-encrusted sword. To Queen Hygd he gave three splendid palfreys with their gold-braided reins, and also the marvelous collar set with priceless and glittering stones. She put it on at once, smiling and holding her head high in her delight with it;

and, though she had been fine to look upon before, every warrior in the hall said that it made her the fairest woman in all the world.

King Hygelac was no less generous than his young warrior. He gave to Beowulf a seat beside him on the high place in his mead hall, and every night the Queen presented the mead cup to Beowulf after she had presented it to her lord. He gave him also broad lands, in which there was farmland and meadow, forest and brook. On that land he built him a castle high enough to be seen from the sea. To all this he added a great heap of gold rings, enough of them to keep Beowulf wealthy and generous all his days.

It is told by the minstrels how Beowulf lived long and happily in his native land. In the years of his life there was peace between the Geats and the Danes, and ships from each land were often anchored without challenge on the other's shore. To King Hygelac and Queen Hygd, he became like a son. To their only child, the Prince of the Geats, he became as an elder brother, advising and guarding him, teaching him the arts of war and the arts of peace.

Long, long afterward, when Beowulf was a man with a graying beard and Hygelac and Hygd were no longer on the earth, the new King of the

Geats met his death in battle. And when the mourning for him was over and the warriors were called together to choose a new lord, they did not question or hesitate. With one voice they elected Beowulf to be their king.

Legacy Books